Adelaide F. (Adelaide Florence) Samuels

**Palm Land**

Or, Dick Travers in the Chagos Islands

Adelaide F. (Adelaide Florence) Samuels

**Palm Land**
*Or, Dick Travers in the Chagos Islands*

ISBN/EAN: 9783337209513

Printed in Europe, USA, Canada, Australia, Japan

Cover: Foto ©Andreas Hilbeck / pixelio.de

More available books at **www.hansebooks.com**

*DICK TRAVERS ABROAD*

---

# PALM LAND

OR

## DICK TRAVERS IN THE CHAGOS ISLANDS

MISS ADELAIDE F. SAMUELS

AUTHOR OF "THE DICK AND DAISY SERIES," "THE LOST TAR, OR
DICK TRAVERS IN AFRICA," "ON THE WAVE, OR DICK TRAV-
ERS ABOARD THE 'HAPPY JACK,'" "LITTLE CRICKET,
OR DICK TRAVERS IN LONDON."

BOSTON 1892
LEE AND SHEPARD PUBLISHERS
10 MILK STREET NEXT "OLD SOUTH MEETING HOUSE"

# Affectionately Dedicated

## To

# WALTER AND CHARLEY BRADLEE.

# CONTENTS.

## CHAPTER VIII.

## CHAPTER IX.

## CHAPTER X.

## CHAPTER XI.

## CHAPTER XII.

## CHAPTER XIII.

# PALM LAND;

## OR,

## DICK TRAVERS IN THE CHAGOS ISLANDS.

---

## CHAPTER I.

### ON DECK.

"All hands! up anchor, a-ho-oy!" was the boatswain's hoarse call; and leaning over the railing on the deck of the "Andromeda," Dick waved his hat to Daisy and grandfather Milly on shore, as that neat little vessel glided smoothly out of Boston harbor.

When the flutterings of the white handkerchiefs on shore could no longer be distinguished, our hero turned his attention to what was going on about him on deck. Sailors were hurrying hither and thither, executing rapidly-given orders that were to him unintelligible; but the sailors themselves received the greatest share of his attention. One, in particular, took Dick's eye, — a jolly, round-faced, fat man, who seemed altogether too fleshy to be able to step about as rapidly as he did; but who looked as though he could spin a "sailor's yarn" to perfection; and Dick inwardly resolved to hear him spin more than one before the end of the voyage.

While occupied thus, our hero became suddenly conscious that some one was scrutinizing him as earnestly as he had scrutinized the sailor; and turning to the right, he saw, seated upon the deck, where he was almost wholly concealed from view by a sail that he had placed dexterously about him, one of the blackest negro boys he had ever seen. His nose was very flat, his lips very thick, and his teeth, every one of which he exhibited as Dick looked at him, were exceedingly white.

"Who are you?" questioned Dick, after a pause, in which he had been viewing with curiosity all that was viewable of the boy.

"I'm Cuffee Dandelion. Nebber heard ob me afore?" replied Cuffee, with another exhibition of his "ivory."

"No, never. What are you doing on board the 'Andromeda?'" interrogated Dick, with a smile at the incredulous expression that came over Cuffee's face, on his declaring he had never heard of. him before.

"I *belong* on board de 'Androm'da,' I do;

been wif it everywhere it's been for the last free years."

" O, you must be quite a good sailor by this time. How happens it I don't see you stirring with the rest of them?"

"Sailor!" repeated Cuffee, contemptuously. " S'pect I'd stoop so low as to be a sailor? I'm captin's mate. Yah, yah! 'Cause why? cause I'm always wif de captin. Dat am why."

" O, you are the captain's cabin-boy. I remember now I've heard him speak of you. You must have learnt lots that is worth knowing, in the years you have been on board the 'Andromeda.'"

" An' lots dat's not worf knowing," added Cuffee.

" How's that? I thought everything was worth knowing," said Dick, taking a seat on a pile of ropes near him.

" For one thing, 't is n't worf knowing how mad our captin can get wif dis chile. Wish I never knowed it," replied Cuffee, seriously.

" O!" said Dick, suspecting the cause of Cuffee's seriousness. " Well, I guess that's the only thing you found not worth knowing."

" An' for another thing," continued Cuffee, as though he had not heard Dick's remark, " it's not worf knowing how it feels to be sea-sick."

" Were you sea-sick?" questioned Dick, who

could not help laughing at the expression upon
Cuffee's face, at the word.

"Golly, sea-sick am no name for it! but you'll
know if it am worf knowing, afore you're fru wif
de 'Androm'da,' for she am de greatest for rolling
you ebber saw."

"Cuffee! Cuffee! Where *is* that boy?" It
was Captain Fairweather's voice; and Cuffee
sprang to his feet, shouting, in reply, —

"Here I is, Massar Captin; I only jus' stopped
a minute to fix dis old sail dat was flopping ober
de deck." And Cuffee hurriedly put the sail in
place just as the captain approached them.

"Go down immediately and put that cabin in
order," said he, with a frown at Cuffee's innocent
face.

"Yes, sar; I was on my way dar, long ago."
And before the captain could say more, his woolly
head had disappeared below.

"That's the laziest boy that it was ever my
misfortune to meet with," said Captain Fairweather, turning to Dick, with a smile. "Do
you think you will enjoy the voyage?"

"Yes, sir; if this is a fair specimen of what I
may expect," replied Dick, looking out upon the
calm water that was red with the light of the
setting sun.

"You can rest assured that it is a *very fair*

specimen," replied the captain, with a smile, as he turned to give some orders to the crew.

Dick stood upon the deck until the sun had gone down behind the land that had always been his home ; then, when neither sun or land could longer be seen, he went below into his state-room, where he made some alterations in his toilet before joining the captain at supper.

# CHAPTER II.

## A MONKEY MERCHANT.

NOTHING occurred on board the " Andromeda " that would interest my young readers until that vessel dropped anchor before the little island of Bravo, one of the Cape Verde Islands, where Captain Fairweather always stopped to take in a fresh supply of provisions.

No sooner was the anchor dropped than canoes, loaded with fruit, vegetables, and poultry, and propelled by either negroes or Portuguese, began to shoot out from the island.

Dick stood on deck watching them, and was soon joined by Cuffee, who, without a word, fixed his eyes upon the shore, and by the expression in them, Dick felt sure he expected to see some one in one of the canoes that he knew; and he was right; for before a minute had passed, Cuffee suddenly exclaimed (and there was anything but pleasure in his face as he did so), —

" Golly!  Dare dey are, sure enough ! "

" Who is it? " interrogated Dick, looking in the direction that Cuffee was looking.

" Can't you see something uncommon in dat boat ober dare, dat's jus' putting away from shore all alone?" said Cuffee, pointing one black finger in the direction indicated.

" The one that is rowed by a man and a boy?" questioned Dick, shading his eyes from the sun with his hand.

" A man an' a *boy?*" repeated Cuffee, contemptuously.

" Yes."

" Golly! I thought you had better eyes 'n dat! Call dat *thing* a boy?"

" O, I see now; it's a monkey!" exclaimed Dick, in surprise; for seated upon the seat, in the approaching boat, beside an old white-haired man, who had but one arm, was a large-sized monkey, who held an oar, and with his comical head on one side to see better the movements of his master, used his oar skilfully, in perfect time with the one in the hand of the old man.

In a few minutes this novel pair were alongside of the " Andromeda," when the monkey threw his oar across the old man's knees, then taking a small bag of fruit from the bottom of the boat, fixed it upon his own back, and began to climb to the deck.

" Well, I never saw anything that could come up to that!" exclaimed Dick, with a laugh, turning to Cuffee ; but Cuffee had suddenly disappeared from his side.

"O, here's Bon!" exclaimed Captain Fairweather, approaching, as the monkey came upon deck and emptied the contents of his bag very near Dick's feet ; then stepping back a step, waited patiently for some of the sailors to buy his fruit.

Dick stooped down, and picking up a large, fresh orange, was about to eat it, when Captain Fairweather interposed, saying, with a laugh, —

"Don't bite it till you have given him a silver piece in exchange, for Bon has a sorry temper, when his property is in danger, and might serve you as he did Cuffee, last year."

"How was that?" interrogated Dick, taking a silver piece from his pocket, and tossing it to the monkey, who caught it dexterously, and tucked it away in the empty bag, then flashed his sharp little eyes around him, to see which hand would throw the next.

"Where is Cuffee?" inquired the captain, without replying to Dick's question, looking among the sailors for the missing cabin-boy.

"He was here a minute ago," replied Dick.

"Ha, ha! He didn't care about seeing Bon, and I can't blame him much. You see, last year, he thought it would be an easy thing to impose upon a monkey, and get his fruit without the customary silver piece ; so he took up an orange, and began to eat it. But Bon had his eyes on him, and as soon as the last mouthful disappeared, he jumped upon Cuffee's back, and bit him severely on the shoulder : he bears the scar to this day."

" No wonder he does n't care about seeing him," observed Dick, with a laugh.

" No wonder, indeed! You never saw such a frightened darkey as he was at the time. His yells could be heard for a mile around."

By this time the sailors had bought all of Bon's fruit on deck, and that lively little merchant had returned to his boat, secured another bag, and was on deck again, waiting to sell out his second stock. This he did equally quick, for the sailors were only too glad to buy of such a comical little merchant, and gave him more than one pat and friendly poke with the silver pieces, all of which Bon received in dignified silence.

Captain Fairweather bought the contents of the third bag, and Dick the fourth ; one more was sold to the sailors ; then Bon's stock was disposed of, and climbing down into his boat he took up his oar, and waited for his master to make the first dip for home, which he did not do until his one hand had patted Bon approvingly upon the back several times.

" He does n't miss his right arm much, with

that monkey to do his work for him," said Captain Fairweather, looking after them.

"How could he learn him to be so useful?" said Dick.

"O, they understand each other perfectly. They have lived together for the last five years, and in all that time the old man has had nothing to think of, or care about, but Bon. I believe he thinks as much of him now as he would of a son; and Bon understands every word he says to him."

"Where have you been, Cuffee?" a sailor was heard to inquire, with a laugh, behind them, at that moment; and the captain and Dick both turned to hear Cuffee's reply, which was, —

"I only jus' went below to sweep out the captin's cabin."

"Mighty industrious all of a sudden. Why didn't you stop on deck, and buy some fruit of Bon? He's grown good-looking since you saw him last," continued the sailor.

"He'd hab to grow mighty handsome to be good-looking in dis chile's eyes; an' I'd rudder not look at him till he is," replied Cuffee, walking up to Dick, as Captain Fairweather turned away, with a smile, to superintend the buying of provisions.

"I was very much pleased with Bon," said our

hero to Cuffee, with a glance after the retreating
boat.

"S'posed you would be," replied Cuffee, shortly.

"Why, don't you like him?" inquired Dick, innocently, with a desire to hear Cuffee tell his own
story.

"O, yes; I lub him so much I'd like to smash
his head in; an' I would, only I should n't like to
leave dat poor one-armed fellar without any pro-
tectar," replied Cuffee, with an angry glance over
the water.

"Why, did he ever hurt you?" Dick continued to question, enjoying Cuffee's excitement im-
mensely.

"Did he eber hurt me?" mimicked Cuffee.
"I'd like to know what you'd call dat?" And
pulling off his jacket, he bared his shoulder for Dick
to see a large red scar, where Bon had bit him.

"O!" exclaimed Dick, surprised, for it was
much larger than he had supposed it would be.
"How did he come to do that?"

"Well, you see dis am de way ob it," said
Cuffee, putting on his jacket again, a little ap-
peased by the sympathy in Dick's voice. "I'd
always bought his fruit till last year, an' paid for
it; but last year I paid for an orange dat, when
I come to eat it, I found was rotten on de inside;
so I jus' grabbed another, so as not to get cheated,

an' when I'd eaten it all up, if dat monkey didn't jump on my back, all of a sudden, an' bite me jus' where you see de scar. Golly! if I didn't tink he was goin' to eat me up, jus' to get back dat orange; an' he would hab done it, too, if it hadn't been for the captin, who came an' waled him over de head wid a bag of his own fruit."

" Is that why you were afraid to come on deck to-day?"

"'*Fraid?* I'll let you know, Massar Dick, dat dis child am afraid of *nuffing.* I didn't want to come up, cause I didn't know but I might kill him when I saw him, close to; den what would become ob dat poor old man, as I said afore?" And Cuffee, with a very serious face, accepted an orange that Dick offered him, and after peeling it dexterously, swallowed it in two mouthfuls.

# CHAPTER III.

## A HOME IN DIEGO GARCIA.

" MASSAR DICK ! Massar Dick ! You jus' come on deck if you want to see fun ! " exclaimed Cuffee, rushing into Dick's state-room, one afternoon, after the " Andromeda " had carried them safely through a fearful storm off the Cape of Good Hope.

" What's on deck that's funny ; another Bon ? " said Dick, throwing down the book he was reading to follow the cabin-boy ; but Cuffee was far ahead, and made no reply.

Upon reaching the deck, Dick saw Cuffee bending over the railing, watching a large bird of the gull species that was in pursuit of a flying-fish ; and upon looking into the water he saw that the flying-fish was there pursued by a larger fish ; so that neither air nor water offered a safe refuge to the pursued.

" Golly ! it 'll be fun to see which ob de two get him ! " exclaimed Cuffee, with shining eyes.

" Which do you think will ? " asked Dick.

" De gull, I guess ; he gener'l'y habs eberyting
his own way."

" Did you ever see anything like it before ? "

" Yes, lots ob times. 'Spect I've been on de
water five years, and neber seen nuffin ? "

" There ! the gull has it now ! " exclaimed
Dick, suddenly, as the bird descended like a shot
over the fish.

" No, not dis time ; but he 'll hab it de next,
sure ; 'cause dat fish am 'bout tired out," replied
Cuffee, as the bird ascended into the air again
without its prey ; and Cuffee's word proved pro-
phetic, for the next time the gull descended it
was seen to bear the flying-fish away in its
talons.

" Doctor," the black cook, now made his appearance upon deck with a fishing-line and hook
nicely baited, which he threw overboard ; and
after waiting patiently for some time, without re-
garding the jeers of the sailors at his unsuccess,
he was so fortunate as to pull upon deck a large
dolphin, which he carried off to his own quarters
in triumph.

Dick declared it was the handsomest fish he
had ever seen, for while life lasted its colors were
very brilliant and changeable ; but as soon as it
was dead, it became dim and lustreless, not a
trace of its beauty remaining.

After dark that night, Captain Fairweather called Dick upon deck to see a strange phenomenon. It appeared to those on board the "Andromeda" as though that brave little vessel was ploughing its way through a sea of fire, so numerous were the *infusoria* that had the power of emitting light, and were often called the glow-worms of the sea.

"What causes it?" questioned Dick, who had never seen anything of the kind before, looking down into the glowing water.

"Very small insects," replied the captain. "You can judge how many there must be, to cause the water to look like that. You never saw anything half so wonderful on land, did you?"

"No, sir; but I should be pleased to see some land, for all that," replied Dick, who was getting tired of sky and water.

"Well, then, prepare to be pleased to-morrow morning; for you will see land then, and go ashore."

Long before daybreak the next morning, Dick was on deck looking for some sign of the promised land; but it was not visible until nearly nine o'clock.

It was the little island of Diego Garcia that the captain intended stopping at; and as they approached it, it seemed to those on the deck of the "Andromeda" as though the waves would wash over it and cover it from view, so low it was upon the water.

It was about half a mile wide, and three miles long; shaped like a crescent, and covered with luxuriant vegetation.

As the " Andromeda " dropped anchor in the bay, a canoe put out from the shore, in which was one white man, and several negroes paddling. The canoe attracted much attention. It was hewn out of iron wood, and was about forty feet long. As it came alongside the "Andromeda," the white man (who proved to be a middle-aged Frenchman, with a very fast tongue, and equally fast motions) came on deck, and after embracing Captain Fairweather, seized his hand and shook it as though he was trying to shake it out of his coat-sleeve.

" Glad to see you, captain! Glad to see you! Come ashore, an' we will have ze grand dinner. Come for oil, eh?"

The captain, who had been equally glad to see him, answered in the affirmative, and after a few minutes of conversation, added that his " young friend would like to go ashore, too," referring to Dick.

" Sartainment! Sartainment! I'm only too glad to welcome any of your friends!" exclaimed the Frenchman, walking up to Dick and shaking his hand in the same manner that he had shaken the captain's.

Captain Fairweather and Dick, after the former had given some directions to the sailors, followed the Frenchman into the boat, and in a short time it grated upon the sandy beach.

Monsieur Barda escorted them to his house (which seemed to have been built with the intention of having it as airy as possible), then went in search of his wife.

It (the house) was constructed almost wholly of rattan and bamboo. Bamboos lashed neatly together formed the sides, and in each of the apertures left for windows was a net-work of rattan. The roof was covered with palm-leaves, and over the veranda many kinds of tropical vines were in blossom, filling the air with a delicious fragrance.

Dick looked about him with curiosity, and was not a little surprised, too, to see that the house was surrounded by fig, cocoa-nut, banana, and many other kinds of fruit-trees.

The Frenchman soon returned with his wife, who welcomed her guests in broken English, and conducted them through the house into the garden, where, within a summer-house, which was made wholly of rattan and bamboo, and covered with luxurious vines, was spread a tempting repast.

In fact, Dick was surprised at the variety of dishes; and in America this dinner would have been considered a treat; but in the Chagos Islands it was an every-day affair.

The "bill of fare" consisted of turtle soup, fricasseed chickens, roast turtle, omelet of turtles' eggs, fried mullet, shrimp sauce, vegetables, and a variety of fruit.

As they entered the summer-house, a little negro girl, with a basket of green cocoa-nuts, entered it through another door. Placing her basket upon the ground, she began to crack the nuts with an iron hook, and to pour the water from them into a pitcher. Dick could only guess they were cocoa-nuts, for they were unlike any he had ever seen in Boston, their shells being a light color, and almost transparent, and full of a cool, pleasant drink, which was used upon the table instead of water.

While the quick-motioned Frenchman was seating his guests, four children entered the summer-house, and seated themselves at the table also. Dick looked at them with curiosity, and received a corresponding look from them. They were the Frenchman's children; and the eldest, a boy of thirteen years, was named Baptiste, of whom we shall have much to say in the future.

# CHAPTER IV.

## HOW THEY MAKE COCOA-NUT OIL.

After dinner, the captain and Monsieur Barda retired to the veranda to talk and smoke ; and on Dick's expressing a wish to walk about and see the island, the Frenchman called Baptiste to him, and bade him show " ze young gentleman ze meels," meaning the mills.

Dick walked by Baptiste's side down to the sea-beach first, where there was a large open shed, under which were many colored women and girls laughing and jabbering together in some unknown tongue.

Each of them had an iron hook, and was busy cracking cocoa-nuts, of which there was a large pile under the shed. Another party of girls and women were taking those that had been cracked, breaking the nuts in halves, and placing them on the beach in the hot sun, while another party of women and girls were removing the meat from those placed on the sand and gathering it up in baskets and throwing it into a large wooden vat.

Dick was curious to know what so much ma-
noeuvring meant; so he asked Baptiste if he would
tell him.

"Ze women under ze shed," replied Baptiste,
who was a healthy-looking, dark-skinned, rosy-
cheeked boy, — "ze women under ze shed cracks
ze nuts, zen za are put in ze hot sun for ze meat
to curl up, so za will come out easy; zen ze meat
is put in the vat to ferment wiz little water."

This reply, given in much more broken English
than I have written it, was accompanied with so
many gestures, that Dick thought the little French
boy must know the deaf and dumb language.

"How long do they keep it in the vat?" Dick
asked, after a short pause.

"Few days, — week."

"What do they do with it then?"

"Come wiz me," was the reply, accompanied
by a characteristic gesture. Dick followed him
to a building which was built not unlike our New-
England corn-barns, with open sides.

"Zis is ze drying-house,' said Baptiste, pointing to it, and opening the door for Dick to see
how it was packed with the meat of the cocoa-nut.

"Where is the mill?" asked Dick. He expected it would be a large building, full of noisy
machinery, the same as many mills he had been
in near Boston. What was his surprise, on step-

ping out from a grove of trees into an open clearing, to see something in the middle of the open ground that looked like a mammoth mortar, holding two or three barrels of cocoa-nut meats. Two asses were driven in a circle by an old white-haired negro, turning a beam which was attached to the mortar. Upright beams were fastened to this, which in turn supported a large pestle, which was thus made to revolve, crushing the oil from the meats. This oil ran into a trough at the base of the mortar. But the cut will show you, much better than I can describe it, the appearance of this mill.

Dick thought a common cider-mill, such as he had seen at home, would answer the purpose much better; but he was too polite to express this opinion; for looking at Baptiste, he saw that he was observing him, with a light in his eye which seemed to say, " Did you ever see anything so grand before? "

From the mill, the oil was conveyed to tanks holding from fifty to an hundred barrels of oil, from which men were pumping oil to take on board the "Andromeda."

As this walk had taken some time, Dick thought they had better return; so Baptiste led the way back to the house

" O, Dick, I have bad news for you! " said

Captain Fairweather, as soon as he stepped upon the vine-covered veranda.

"Bad news!" repeated Dick.

"Yes. My good friend, Monsieur Barda, informs me that the cholera is raging fearfully in Calcutta"

"That is bad news, indeed."

"For myself I am not afraid, for I am a tough, weather-beaten old sailor; but for you I have fears. I should never dare to face my old friend · Mr. Milly again, if anything should happen to you while under my care. Don't you think it would be the best plan — I am sure it would be the safest — to remain with Monsieur Barda until my return? He will do everything to make you have a pleasant time, and there are many sources of amusement on the island. Come, now, don't you think you had better remain here for a few weeks, than to spend that time on the water, with only three or four days in Calcutta, where everything is running wild?"

Dick paused a moment, undecided, till catching the eye of Baptiste, which seemed to express a wish for him to remain, he replied, —

"I think I had."

"I am glad of that, and I am sure you will not repent of your decision. I will leave a letter with you for the American consul here, as a precaution in case anything should happen to prevent my return."

At this moment Monsieur's wife appeared and informed them that supper was waiting.

# CHAPTER V.

### THE SERENADE.

AFTER supper, Monsieur informed the captain that in honor of their arrival, there would be " ze grand serenade " that evening.

This information made Dick anxious to know who the musicians would be, as he had seen no one on the island, as yet, but the Frenchman's family and the negroes, who lived in little huts near the beach.

" Where are the musicians?" he asked of Baptiste, as they sat on the veranda together after supper.

" Ze *what?*" inquired Baptiste; who, as the question would not admit of a gesture with his hand, gesticulated with his eyebrows, bringing them close together in a manner which signified that he did not understand.

Dick, thinking that he was unacquainted with the word " musician," tried to simplify his question by saying, " Who will make the music this evening?"

How they make Cocoa-nut Oil. — Page 29.

"O!" replied Baptiste, bringing his eye-brows in place, and smiling; "ze negroes will make ze music. See, zey are getting ready."

Dick looked in the direction that Baptiste pointed, and saw some twenty negroes, men and boys, bringing basket after basket of cocoa-nut shells, and throwing them in a pile, which soon appeared like a small mountain.

"What is that for?" asked Dick.

"Zat will be ze grand fire."

"A bonfire of cocoa-nut shells?"

"Yes."

At eight o'clock, the other members of the Frenchman's family and the captain came out on the veranda, and in a few moments after, a flame of fire was seen to shoot up from the pile of shells, then others darted from it in every direction, until the whole mass was on fire, sending a brilliant light far into the grove of tropical trees, startling the birds that had gone to rest, and caus-ing them to fly wildly about, while many darted into the flames and perished.

Soon negro men and women began to come up in groups, until thirty or forty had assembled on the open space, or lawn, before the French-man's house.

Then three negro men appeared, each with a large drum, eleven feet long, made of a hollow

3

trunk of a tree, one end of which was open, the other covered with skin. Each of these drums, as they lay on their their sides, were raised upon blocks; and upon each a negro drummer seated himself astraddle, and began to drum with his fists, and at every beat to howl something in the Madagascar language; for they were all natives of Madagascar, and were formerly slaves in the isles of France, but were now liberated by the English government.

All the men and women then formed into a large circle, and squat down, or sat on their heels, clapping their hands, and singing and shouting. While they were singing, a large, fleshy negro woman, named Venus, whom Baptiste told Dick was the champion dancer, sprang into the circle; she was dressed in a red calico dress, and her head was ornamented with a huge red turban.

Taking a gliding step to the time of the chorus, her movements at first were slow, and gradually became more rapid; and at apparently a challenge from her, a large black man jumped into the ring and joined her in the dance; and for fifteen minutes their chief object seemed to be to excel each other in rapidly moving their limbs.

At last the man retired, amid shouts and hoots from his companions, thoroughly tired out; the perspiration rolling down his cheeks in great beads. But Venus, to Dick's amusement, continued the dance, without slackening her speed in the least, and was soon joined by another negro. Not till she had tired him, also, did she condescend to leave the ring, then apparently not in the least fatigue 1.

Upon her exit, another took her place, and so the dance was kept up, accompanied by drumming, clapping of hands, and hooting or singing, until Dick's amusement began to change to weariness. Eleven o'clock, and he began to doze in his chair; by half-past eleven the bonfire appeared to be nearer, and the negroes seemed to be horrible demons, yelling and dancing in the very midst of the flames.

He was beginning to grow very uneasy, when the captain's voice, saying, "It's over now," brought him to his senses. Sitting up in his chair and rubbing his eyes, he saw the negroes moving slowly away, headed by those bearing the drums; and soon nothing remained of the *serenade* but a heap of live coals where the bonfire had blazed.

Monsieur Barda then led his guests to their sleeping apartments; and Dick, after saying his prayers, was soon in a sound sleeep. So passed his first day and night on the island.

After breakfast the next morning, Monsieur

Barda rowed the captain to the ship, and Dick went with the boat, for he had expressed a desire to bid Cuffee good-by.

Poor Cuffee was greatly disappointed when he was told that Dick would remain on the island until the ship returned from Calcutta.

"Golly, if dat ain't meaner dan making me a nigger!" he exclaimed, with an expression of deep woe. "I tot dat you were going de whole voyage."

"So I did intend to. But Captain Fairweather wants me to remain, because the cholera is raging there fearfully."

"De cholera!" exclaimed Cuffee, showing the whites of his eyes to an alarming extent.

"Yes."

"Say, Massa Dick. Could n't you 'duce de captain to let dis chile stay on de island too?" This Cuffee said in a very low tone, with his lips close to Dick's ear.

"I am afraid not, Cuffee. I hinted as much on the way to the ship, and he said that he could n't do without you."

"Could n't do without me! He calls me de laziest nigger he ever set eyes on. Golly, if he don't hab cause to call me dat before we reach Calcutta!"

"Why, Cuffee?"

" 'Spect I 's goin' to work all de way, an' *den* die wid de cholera?"

" Are you afraid of the cholera?"

" 'Fred of it?  Dis chile is 'fred of nuffing ; an' 'cause I *won't* be 'fred of it, dat 'll be jus' why it 'll come at me, an' gobble me up all de fiercer."

" I am sorry to hurry you, Dick ; but ' a fair wind is blowing, and we must away,' " said the captain, approaching Dick with a smile, and extending his hand.  " Good-by ; and may you have a pleasant time on the island   You will see the ship again before many weeks have passed away."

" Good-by, sir ; and may *you* have a pleasant voyage.  Good-by, Cuffee."

' Good-by, Massa Dick.  You 'll nebber see dis poor darkey again," replied Cuffee, ready to blubber.

" Why, what does the little fellow mean?" asked the captain of Dick, in surprise.

" I think, sir, he is afraid of catching the cholera," replied Dick.

" Afraid of the cholera !  The cholera won't trouble you, Cuffee, so long as you follow your nose to do your duty ; that 's certain "

" 'Spect it would n't, Massa Captin, if dis chile had such a big nose as you hab to follow   Golly, *would n't* it protec' me !" replied Cuffee, spite fully, looking hard at the captain's nose, which was larger than the ordinary size.

The captain seemed undecided whether to be angry or to laugh at this retort. At last, putting on a stern face, he ordered the offender below, which was the greatest punishment he could put upon him, as he wanted to watch Dick going ashore.

After bidding the captain good-by again, Dick joined Monsieur Barda in his boat; and sitting so that he could see the ship, he watched those on board making preparations to start again on her voyage.

Then he began to realize that for six weeks, perhaps longer, he must remain upon that strange island with people whom he knew nothing about, and, until the day before, had not heard of; and he almost began to repent of having given his consent to remain, when Monsieur Barda's pleasant voice interrupted his thoughts.

The Frenchman mistrusted what he was thinking about, and began to talk very fast.

" There is Baptiste," said he, seeing his boy waiting for them on the beach. " Can you sweem?" continued he, turning to Dick and resting on his oars.

" No, sir; I cannot swim. I have often thought I should like to learn," was the reply.

" You wants to see Baptiste sweem ? "

Dick replied in the affirmative ; and Monsieur beckoned to his boy, who seemed to understand him, for he threw off his jacket and bounded into the surf.

" He surely cannot swim to us ! " said Dick, in surprise, for they were many rods from shore.

" We shall see ! " replied Monsieur Barda, with a satisfied shrug of his shoulders.

Dick watched the boy as he came nearer and nearer. In a few minutes he was alongside of the boat, and scrambled into it, dripping wet, his face flushed and smiling.

" Baptiste shall learn Deck how to sweem," said the Frenchman, nodding to his boy, and taking up his oars again.

" Is your name Deck ? " asked Baptiste, seating himself beside our hero.

" Yes," replied Dick, smiling at the boy's pronunciation.

" We shall be grand friends, Deck. I am glad you will stay."

In a short time the Frenchman ran the boat upon the sandy beach, and Dick said to himself, —

" My new life has really begun."

# CHAPTER VI.

### A STRANGE PET.

"Where are they going, Baptiste?" said Dick, as he stepped from the boat, and noticed about twenty negro men starting down the harbor, each in a little canoe, and each having a hard-wood stick and a basket.

"Zey are going for ze cocoa-nuts."

"Going for cocoa-nuts in boats?" observed Dick, incredulously.

"Zey will go ashore farzer down ze island."

"O, that's it. And I suppose each man has to get his basket full of cocoa-nuts?"

"Each man mus' get his basket full many times. Every day he mus' get four hundred, or he no get pay."

"How would any one know it, if he did n't get four hundred?"

"My farzer counts zem."

"I should think that would be a tiresome job. Why, that would make him have eight thousand cocoa-nuts to count every day, if there are twenty men and each man gets four hundred. I should think it would take him all day to count them."

" No ; only one — two — three minutes. I will show you to-night, when zey all come back, how we count ze cocoa-nuts."

" I should n't think they would last long, going at the rate of eight thousand a day."

" All ze time zey lasts. Ze trees blossom an' bear all ze time. You will see ze blossom by ze side of ze full-grown nut."

" In America, trees have more regularity about them " replied Dick, smiling. " Why, if one of the trees in my father's old apple-orchard should have had blossoms and fruit upon it at the same time, my father would have cut it down, as a tree that did n't have common-sense. But you did n't tell me what the men carry the hard-wood sticks for."

" Zat is to knock off ze outside bark of ze nuts ; ze bark we use, too, to make ropes an' mats. Now, I will show you my leetle pet."

Dick followed him to a grove of orange-trees, where there was a cage upon the ground, in which was a pet chameleon. Around the cage were gathered Baptiste's sisters and brother, and Baptiste, with true French politeness, began to introduce them to Dick.

" Zis is Marie," said he, introducing his dark-haired and black-eyed sister, who was eleven years old, and who held in her hand a box full of insects that she had caught for the chameleon.

As she had never seen a white boy to speak to, except her own brothers, before she saw Dick, of course she did not know what to say to him; so she only bestowed upon him a side glance, as she put a beetle upon a flat stick for the chameleon.

The next one introduced was Baptiste's eight-year-old brother Jean; who, upon being introduced, seemed to think he was too near the stranger, and so moved away to the other side of the cage. The next and last was little Finnette, who, being the youngest and most petted, was of course afraid of no one; and she looked at Dick with great fearless black eyes, while he patted her rosy cheek.

After Dick had been introduced to them all, they turned their attention to the chameleon.

He was about six inches long, with very flat sides; his skin was very rough, or covered with little points like shagreen; and the light reflected from the points made his color similar to the inside of a brilliant shell.

In a strong light he seemed to be all colors, the most prominent one being green; but in a dim light he was a dull brown.

The most curious thing about him, Dick thought, was the manner he could turn his prominent eyes about, without regard to each other. One eye would be looking at Jean, while the other was looking at Marie, in a very different direction. Or one eye would be turned up, while the other was turned down; but they were scarcely ever together, as eyes should be.

"Hold zat so far off," said Baptiste to Dick, giving him the flat stick, with a beetle struggling upon his back, on it. Dick advanced the stick till the beetle was within six inches of the chameleon, when the latter darted out his long tongue, and the beetle was gone in a flash.

The children all looked at Dick, when the beetle disappeared, to see if he would be surprised; but he was not, for he had often seen toads, in the garden at home, catch flies and other insects in the same manner.

After watching the chameleon for some time longer, Baptiste led Dick to the garden behind the house to show him the bee-hives, which consisted of two hollow trees, resting upon two others similar to common chopping blocks.

While they were looking at them, an old negro woman made her appearance, and straightway Baptiste began to jump and dance, and appeared greatly pleased about something.

On the contrary, the old colored woman appeared anything but pleased on seeing Baptiste, and shaking her fist at him, she turned and walked away a few steps, as though she would go back again in the direction she had come.

At this, Baptiste laughed outright, and taking Dick's hand, said, "Come this way, Deek."

"Who is it, Baptiste; and what did she shake her fist at you for?" asked Dick, much surprised.

"Zat is old Aunt Stagger, ze cook. She is going for honey, an' is mad for I see her."

"Mad because you saw her?"

"Yes."

"Why?"

"She knows zat I know she will make ze honey cakes; an' she tinks I will eat zem faster zan she can make zem. Ha, ha!"

Dick laughed too, now that he knew what caused the old woman to put on such a savage face.

"I thought she was crazy," said he, "and was looking for a stick to defend myself with, in case she should attack us."

"O, no; she nezer hurts any one. She is only lazy. She no wants to cook so many as I wants to eat; ha, ha! Come, let's go to the cook-house before she gets there."

Dick followed the boy to an old house which was stowed with boxes and barrels full of provisions, and in which all the cooking was done for Monsieur Barda's table.

After dragging Dick after him between some barrels, and behind a table upon which was a pan of light batter, and some cooking utensils, Baptiste put his finger to his lips to caution Dick to keep silent ; and Dick began to feel very much like a thief as he waited there, afraid to speak ; but Baptiste seemed to be greatly delighted.

At last a shuffling step was heard outside, and old Aunt Stagger appeared in the door-way. She evidently expected to see some one, for, with a frightful scowl upon her face, she flashed a look all round the cook-house ; then, apparently convinced that no one was there besides herself, she put a dish of honey upon the table with a satisfied grunt.

Dick could easily see all that she did without betraying himself ; and with much curiosity he watched her take down a bamboo machine, which was not unlike a syringe, inside of which was a smaller one. The smaller one she filled with honey, and the larger one she filled with light batter from the pan on the table. Then, after raking the fire in the chimney-place to make the kettle of boiling fat that was hanging over it still hotter, she began to play the contents of the machine into the hot fat, making whirligig cakes, which were full of

honey ; all the while keeping her face towards the
door, that no one should enter it without her
knowledge, and bear off the cakes which, as fast
as they were done, she put in a dish upon the table.

Baptiste waited until the dish was **nearly full,**
then, after gesticulating to Dick to follow him
carefully, he took the dish, and keeping a comical look fixed on Aunt Stagger, began to creep
stealthily from his hiding-place towards the door.

The old cook saw him before he was through
it ; but before she could reach him, he darted out
and away, with a loud whoop, followed by Dick.

Looking back, the two boys saw Aunt Stagger
shaking her fists after them, in a manner that
would soon tire her, so she would not be able to
make any more cakes that day.

Baptiste laughed till the tears ran down his
cheeks, while he divided the cakes with Dick. The
latter could not help joining him in the laugh,
though he thought his companion's conduct had
not been quite fair towards the old cook, and
would have told him so, had he been a little more
acquainted with him.

Late that afternoon, they went down to the
beach to see the boats come in laden with cocoa-
nuts. By sunset all the men had returned, and
Monsieur Barda came down to count the nuts.
The way he did it was as follows : —

The boats were in a line along the beach; every man stood up in his boat, and, at a sign from Monsieur, each man threw upon the beach four cocoa-nuts; so, as there were twenty men, the Frenchman was able to count eighty at one throw. Thus he simplified his work greatly.

That evening Dick remained in the house, and became better acquainted with the other members of the Frenchman's family.

He brought down some books from his trunk, which were full of pictures, and with which they all were greatly delighted, not only the children, but Monsieur Barda and his wife, for it was seldom they had the pleasure of seeing a book of any kind.

Neither the children nor their mother could read; and Monsieur himself hesitated long over many of the words. So Dick, to please them, read aloud; and as he had a fine voice, and was not a bad reader, the evening passed away very pleasantly.

Dick's reading aloud settled his position with the children. They looked upon him, while he was reading, with curiosity and wonder; and were firmly convinced that he was the most wonderful boy living; and congratulated themselves that he would have to-remain there a month at least.

# CHAPTER VII.

### BAPTISTE'S IGNORANCE.

THE next morning, Dick asked Baptiste to go with him along the sea-beach, to gather some of the beautiful shells he had seen there, to take home to Daisy.

While they were filling a basket with the handsomest ones, Dick noticed some curious little soft crabs that were running about the sand as though they were seeking something, and were terribly frightened because they could not find it.

"What is the matter with them, Baptiste?" said he

"Put down one of ze shells, an' you will see," was the reply.

Dick took one of the shells from the basket and put it upon the sand. Immediately one of the crabs popped into it. and was seen no more.

"Zat is ze matter; he wants ze house."

"Do they belong in these shells?"

"No; zey go in zem to get away from ze big bird, ze tern, zat eats zem up."

" I suppose they always stay in a shell after they find one."

" No ; zey grow ver' fast. Zat shell soon is too small ; zen he will pop out to see if ze bigger one is near. Zen anozer pops in, an' he has no place to go, an' he will be 'fraid, an' run all round queeck an' crooked."

Dick laughed at this reply, which was, as usual, accompanied by many gestures, and began to gather shells again, looking in every one he took up to see if a crab was in it.

Soon Baptiste called his attention to two birds which were hovering over the water.

" Do you know what zey are?" asked Baptiste.

" No," was the reply.

" Ze lowest one is ze gull ; ze ozer is ze frigate-bird."

At that moment the gull darted down to the water, rising again immediately with a fish in his beak ; when the frigate-bird flew at him, and pecked him till he was glad to drop the fish and fly away.

Before the fish could touch the water, however, the frigate-bird caught it, and bore it away in triumph.

" That was well done," said Dick, turning to Baptiste, after both the birds had disappeared.

" Zat's ze way zey always do. Ze frigate-bird

4

is too lazy to catch fish for himself; so he watch till ze gull catch one, zen he take it away."

"It seemed to me that it was harder for the frigate-bird to take it away than it was for the gull to catch it. I wonder why they don't catch their own fish?"

"So ze fish who may see you walking on ze land may wonder why you don't walk in ze water, it's so much easier," replied Baptiste, with a shrug of his shoulders.

"I suppose you mean by that, that it is easier for the frigate-bird to take the fish away, because it's his nature to do so."

"Zat is it. He could no more catch one in ze water zan you could walk on ze water."

"But I *can* walk on the water, and have often done it at home, in *winter*," replied Dick, laughing.

"Eh? What you say?"

"I say I have often walked on the water." And Dick looked at Baptiste to see if he did not understand that he meant when it was frozen over.

"I no means to *sweem*. I means to stand up straight an' walk "

"That's what I mean. To walk as I am walking now." And Dick took two or three steps to illustrate.

"You can?"

" Yes."

" Let me see you," said Baptiste, pointing to the ocean.

" O, but there's no ice on it now."

" Eh? No eyes?"

" No ice. It isn't frozen over. Don't you know what ice is?"

Baptiste shook his head.

" Why, don't you know that when the weather is cold it makes water hard so that you can cut it?"

" Or walk on it?"

" Yes."

" It's never so here."

" No; it is never so here, because this island is in the torrid zone, and my home is in the temperate zone, where the winters are cold; and when people go out, unless they bundle up warm, they will freeze to death, and be hard too, like the water."

Baptiste shook his head again, and looked at the water. It was evident he was wondering how it could become hard enough to walk upon

Dick suddenly thought of a book that he had in his trunk, which was full of winter scenes; and telling Baptiste to remain where he was a moment, he ran towards the house, soon returning with the book.

" Now, Baptiste," said he, all out of breath with running, " now I will show you a picture of ice. Where can we find a good seat?"

Baptiste took up the basket of shells and led the way from the beach, where it was becoming intensely hot, to a grove of trees. And placing a dead log that lay upon the ground in a better position for a seat, he sat down upon it, and Dick followed his example.

Baptiste watched the book with sparkling eyes, as Dick turned over the leaves. The picture was soon found, and placing the book on Baptiste's knees, Dick bade him look at it well.

It was a picture of a merry party of men, women, and children on the ice skating.

" What does it look like?" asked Dick.

" Many people."

" Yes ; but what are they doing?"

" Dancing ze new dance?"

" O, no ; they are not dancing. They are skating on the ice. That is ice that is under their feet, or water made hard by the cold. You see those things that are strapped to their feet? Those are called skates. On them they can glide over the ice very fast. See, some have fallen down ! That is because they don't know how to skate, and the ice is so slippery they can't stand up."

"What is zat ze lady has?"

"That is a muff. She puts her hands in it to keep them warm."

"What makes all ze trees dead?"

"They are not dead."

"Zare is no leaves upon zem."

"That is because it is winter. The cold weather kills all the leaves, and they fall off; but they come again, fresh and green, in the spring. You should see the trees in autumn, just before the leaves are ready to fall. You never saw such a sight here."

"Why?"

"What would you say if you should get up some morning and see bright red and yellow and brown leaves on all the trees?"

"Did you ever see zem so?"

"Many times. As soon as the frost comes, there is very little green to be seen in the woods; bright, glowing colors take its place. Then, to walk through the woods on a bright, sunshiny day, is almost like walking through fairy-land."

"It must be ze beautiful country."

"It *is* a beautiful country; but the people there get used to all the changes, and let them pass by without a thought."

"What makes ze ground all white?"

"That is because it is covered with snow. Don't you know what snow is?"

Baptiste shook his head.

"Your father must know. Did n't he ever tell you?"

"No," was the reply.

Dick, who, the day before, would not have believed there was such an ignorant boy in the world, began to tell him that "in cold weather the rain freezes up in the air, and comes to the ground in little white flakes, as light as feathers. And," continued he, "we have to dig paths through it, for sometimes it covers the ground as high as my head; and farther north, houses are buried under it, and it is often days before the people can dig their way out."

Baptiste heard this reply in wonder, and Dick turned to the next picture to show how snow came down.

"There! that's the way a snow-storm looks. See how full the air is of little white flakes."

"An' ze boys, too."

"Yes, the boys are covered with it too. They are coasting. Of course you don't know what coasting means, so I will tell you. You see that one that is dragging something up the hill; that is a sled. As soon as he gets to the top of the hill, he will sit down on it, and away he will go, and have a good long ride the whole length of the hill, as that boy is having."

" An' nobody dragging him?"

" No; the snow is slippery after it has been tramped down, and the sled goes itself."

" Zat must be grand fun! How I should like to be zare. Tell me some more about your country."

" I will; and, in turn, you must tell all about this island that I do not know already."

" I will do zat, an' take you all over it before you go away. Ah, you don't know all about it yet. I will take you in among ze cocoa-nut trees. Zare is danger zare."

" Danger?"

" Yes; ze nuts get ripe an' drop to ze ground; an' zey fall from so high, one would kill you if it fell on your head. I was under one once, an' I saw ze big rat up ze tree, an' I tries to kill him, an' ze big nut fell ver' near."

" Do rats go up cocoa-nut trees?"

" Yes; ze big rats from ze ships go up ze trees an' eat ze young nuts. Zare are many rats, too; an' if ze men no kill zem, zare would be no cocoa-nuts."

" That is as new to me as the snow was to you. But here we have another picture. I don't think there are many boys in the world who don't know what that is a picture of."

" More boys," said Baptiste.

" Yes ; but what are they doing?"

" Pulling somezing from ze sky."

Dick laughed heartily at this reply, as any of my young readers would have done ; for it was a picture of boys, flying a kite.

" What d) you do here for amusement? You can't coast, don't know what flying a kite means, and I suppose marbles are Greek to you, too." Baptiste shook his head as though everything Dick had said was Greek to him ; and, pointing to the picture, wanted to know what it was.

" It's a kite," replied Dick ; " boys at home make them to fly in the air."

" What for?"

" Why, for fun. What do you do here for fun?"

" Feesh, sweem, row, an' hunt ze birds an' turtles."

" We do all that in America, and many other things besides. Would you like to know what flying a kite means?"

" Ver' much."

" If you will get me some paste and some slats of wood, I will make one, and we will fly it."

Baptiste hurried away for the slats and paste, and Dick went to his trunk for some old papers to cover the frame with ; and in less than ten minutes from the time he mentioned it, he was busy at work upon it.

Baptiste, while going for the wood and paste, had met his sisters and brother, and had told them that "Deek would make somezing for fun zat he could pull down from ze sky."

So all four of the Frenchman's children clustered around Dick, as he worked, their handsome dark faces bright with anticipation.

The kite was soon finished, and Dick, followed by the children, carried it to the beach, to dry in the hot sun. Then a difficulty arose about flying it that he had not thought of before. It was a hot, sultry day, and not a breath of wind was stirring to carry it up. This he was obliged to explain to his companions, who looked their dis-appointment, but said nothing.

Later in the afternoon, however, a light breeze passed over the island, from the ocean, and the kite was immediately called upon to distinguish itself by being the first one ever flown upon the island.

After a few manœuvres that all boys under-stand, to make it catch the wind, Dick had the gratification of seeing it soaring up nearly out of sight.

Never did a kite behave so well before, and never was he so anxious that it should,

"Now, Baptiste, what do you think of it?" said he, after the string had all been played out, and nothing remained to be done but to hold it.

"It is like ze picture," was the reply. "I wish you could make — what you call?"

"Ice?" prompted Dick.

"Yes. I wish you could make eyes to show me, too."

Dick said he was sorry that he was not able to do that, also, and asked Baptiste if he would not like to hold the string. He took it readily, and after holding it with much pleasure a few moments, passed it to his sisters, who uttered little cries of surprise because it "pulled."

Soon strange cries were heard above them, and looking up, they saw many gulls and frigate-birds rushing through the air towards the kite.

Dick took the string from Marie, and wound it till the kite was half-way down, then paused to see what the birds would do; wondering if one of them would be bold enough to go through it. They repeatedly darted to it, then away, uttering wild cries the while, but all appeared to be afraid to touch it; and on Dick's suddenly letting the string out again they all flew away, screaming fearfully.

"Ha, ha!" laughed Baptiste, "zey could n't find out what kind of bird zat was."

That evening the little French children's tongues flew fast; Baptiste told all that Dick had told him about ice, and the picture-book was brought out again, and it drew as many exclamations of surprise from the other children as it had from him.

Snow and ice were nothing new to Monsieur Barda; but he, like many other fathers, could never find time to give his children a little information about so uninteresting a subject as *the world we live upon.*

# CHAPTER VIII.

### A WALK ACROSS THE ISLAND.

" Now, Baptiste, what shall we do to-day?" said Dick, the next morning.

" We will take ze long walk."

" Yes; that will be splendid, for I want to see more of the island. Who lives on it besides your folks?"

" Nobody."

" Nobody? Then you never have a chance to go visiting, do you?"

" O, yes. My fazer often goes to ze next island in ze boat, to see his friend, Monsieur Bois-blanc. Perhaps he may take you some day."

" I should like to go very much. How far is it?"

" Not ver' far. But look; you sees zat?"

" Yes; it is a black beetle," replied Dick, look-in; down to the foot of a tree, where Baptiste pointed.

" An' do you see zat?" said Baptiste again, pointing in the air to a steel-colored wasp that was flying about in a circle.

" Yes," replied Dick, again.

" Well, now we will wait, an' I tinks you will see somezing zat you never saw in America."

Dick waited patiently by Baptiste's side, watching the wasp and the beetle. The latter jogged along leisurely for a time, till the wasp alighted upon the ground beside it.

" Now what you tinks zat wasp will tell ze beetle?" said Baptiste.

" Will he tell him anything?" asked Dick, laughing at Baptiste's earnest manner while putting such a strange question.

" I tinks he will. I watch zem every day, an' I tinks ze wasp tells ze beetle zat he will lead him up ze tree to one nice dead bird for him to eat, or something like zat; for he *will* lead ze beetle up ze tree, an' he will no try to get away. Now see him!" The wasp had taken hold of the beetle with her mandibles, and began to walk backward with him up the trunk of the tree, the beetle apparently following willingly enough.

After he had led him up the trunk three or four feet, the wasp let go of him, and began to walk slowly around, reconnoitring him; and then, seemingly satisfied, walked up the tree alone.

" She has gone," said Dick.

" Yes; but she will come back. She has gone to find ze good *grave* for ze poor beetle, where ze wind nor ze rain can't throw him to ze ground."

" Find a grave? What do you mean? "

" Wait; you shall see."

In about two minutes the wasp returned and led the beetle farther up the tree, pushed him into a corner between some branches, and deposited her eggs in him, then flew away."

" Zat is ze last of ze poor beetle," said Baptiste.

" Why, won't he leave the corner?" asked Dick.

" Never. Ze wasp has laid her eggs in him, an' by an' by ze eggs will hatch, and ze little wasps will eat him up. I have said, ' What makes him follow ze wasp?' many times, an' could get no answer," continued Baptiste, shaking his head in a puzzled manner. And well may he have been puzzled; for it is a strange fact in Natural History that has puzzled older and wiser heads than his. The most reasonable supposition, however, is, that the beetle had been rendered docile by being poisoned by the wasp when she placed her mandibles upon him.

" Now, Deck," said Baptiste, after they had walked from the tree, — " now, Deck, we will pass through ze woods where zare are many birds, an' we must have steeks."

" What must we have sticks for?" asked Dick.

" Ha, ha! You not know? Well, you shall see," was the reply; and Baptiste left Dick, returning in a moment with two hard-wood sticks in his hand, each about the size of an ordinary cane.

A short walk brought them to the woods, which were thickly grown with underbrush; and as they were trying to force their way through it, cries of alarm were heard among the birds overhead.

" Zey see us now!" said Baptiste. At that moment a species of tern, which was white, and the size of a pigeon, flew in front of him, and lifting his stick, he killed it with one blow.

" O, Baptiste! what made you do that?" cried Dick, horrified at such a cold-blooded proceeding. But before the words were well out of his mouth, he heard a " whiz" in the air, and felt something strike against his face with such force that he nearly fell to the ground, and for a moment he was blinded.

As soon as he could collect his scattered senses he looked about him, and saw Baptiste in the act of striking another bird.

Comprehending the state of affairs immediately, he grasped his own stick tightly, and held it ready for use.

He did not have to wait long before another

white bird flew towards him; and he killed it with as little remorse as Baptiste killed those that flew at him.

"Ha, ha!" laughed the latter, seeing Dick's movements. "Now you know, Deek, what we take ze steeks for."

With the birds and the briars to hinder, it was slow work getting through the woods; but at last they heard the welcome sound of waters, and after pushing through some low bushes, they saw the waves of the Indian Ocean rolling in.

It was an intensely hot day. While they had been going through the woods, they had been well sheltered from the sun's rays; but here, on the open beach, old Sol had full sway; and they were glad to seek what little shade a small cocoa-nut tree, that grew near the bushes, afforded.

"What made the birds fly at us?" said Dick, after they were seated.

"Zey have nests in ze trees, an' zey fear for zare young."

"Birds are not so smart in New England; if they were, boys would not be so fond of robbing their nests."

"Are zare many boys in New England?" asked Baptiste.

"More than I would want to count," replied Dick, laughing.

" More zan all ze men an women on ze island?"

" More than all the men and women, and all the birds and trees too."

" Yes? Where do zey all go?" asked Baptiste, whose eyes grew very big at this reply; and who thought house-room enough could not be found for so many.

" Do you mean, where do they all live?" asked Dick.

" Yes," was the reply.

" Why, they live in houses, with their fathers and mothers. New England is a large place; it would hold hundreds of islands like this, and have room enough left for all the boys."

" How do zey all live? You have no cocoa-nut trees, you say."

" But we have cocoa-nuts though," replied Dick, laughing.

" Ah! zat's it," replied Baptiste, who had been wondering if so many people could live without cocoa-nuts. Then, looking proudly at the small tree beside him, he said, " you have no tree in zat great country so good as zat "

" But we have some that we are very proud of. The oak-tree, for instance," replied Dick.

" Can you make ze house of it?"

" Yes, and many more things."

" Does it give you food when you are hungry?"

5

" No."

" Drink, if you are thirsty ?"

" No."

" Can you make mats from it, or ropes, or dishes?"

" No," replied Dick again.

" An' you calls it as good as ze cocoa-nut tree. Ha, ha ! "

Dick made no reply to this, for he saw that Baptiste was as proud of the island, and its produce, as he himself was proud of New England. He would be a strange boy, indeed, who did not feel proud of his own country.

# CHAPTER IX.

## A SURPRISE.

WHILE they were talking, unknown to them a negro boy had been approaching them, slowly and cautiously at first, dodging in and out of the bushes, and stopping every rod or two to see if he could distinguish their faces ; at last he seemed satisfied, and stepped boldly and joyfully out upon the beach, then ran eagerly towards them.

Dick and Baptiste sprang to their feet at the sight of him, but their faces expressed different emotions. Baptiste's merely expressed curiosity ; Dick's, unbounded astonishment.

The boy still advanced towards them, and when within two or three feet, cried out, —

" O, golly ! Massa Dick, am dat you? I tot I should neber set eyes on you again."

Dick in his astonishment could only articulate one word, —

" Cuffee ! "

" Yes, dis am Cuffee ; likewise it's all dat's left ob him," was the reply.

It was indeed Cuffee, considerably thinner than when we saw him last, however; and his face had lost the care-for-nothing expression that was habitual to it.

"Why, Cuffee! How in the world did you come to be here? I thought you were half-way to China!" exclaimed Dick, at last.

"Wah, yah! I guess not, if dis darkee knows hisself," replied Cuffee, shaking his head.

"Did Captain Fairweather put you ashore after I left the ship? And why did n't you come to Monsieur Barda's house where I am stopping?"

"No, de captin did n't put me ashore; de waves did."

"What do you mean?"

"I mean dat when de captin sent me down in de cabin dat day, I got mad, 'cause dare was no reason why I could n't stay wid you, an' dare was no sense in my goin' where de cholera am; so I tot to myself dat I would jus' jump out ob de cabin window an' swim ashore, an' dey would neber miss me till dey were way out to sea. But after I jumped into de water, I could n't tell which way de land was, so I swam round every way for a time, den I did n't know nuffin' till I found myself lying on de beach here; an' I have been here eber since."

"Poor Cuffee! If I had known that you were

so afraid of the cholera that you had rather jump overboard than run the risk of taking it, I should have tried harder to get the captain to consent to your staying with me," said Dick, compassionately, wondering how Cuffee had escaped drowning.

"Who said I was *'fraid?* I jumped overboard 'cause I *pitied* de cholera. Dat's it. 'Spect I wanted to tempt it to murder *me*, when it's got so many murders to answer for already?"

"There's some philosophy in that, Cuffee," replied Dick, smiling.

"Filusafle! I guess dare am."

"But why did n't you cross the island and join me at Monsieur Barda's?"

"How was I to know where I was? When I opened my eyes. I was on de beach, an' it was dark, an' I heard de most dreadful noise! Golly, was n't it de most awful noise I ebber heard in my life! Fust I tot it was some wild beast, till I climbed to de top ob a high tree, an' looked round an' saw a great fire burning in de distance, an' round it men an' women were dancin' an' yellin' like so many steam-engines."

"It was ze serenade," interrupted Baptiste.

"Den I tot," continued Cuffee, not noticing the interruption, — "den I tot to myself dat I had been washed ashore on a cannibal island, an' de men an' women were cannibals, an' dey were roasting some poor pusson in de fire to eat. Golly! I nebber felt so uncomf'table in my life." And Cuffee wiped the perspiration from his face, that the recollection of that scene had started, with his jacket-sleeve.

"You *did* feel uncomfortable, then!" said Dick. laughing to think that he had admitted it.

"Ob course I felt uncomf'table. How was I to know but, if dey *were* cannibals, one ob dem might spy *me*, an' take me, an' claim me for a *long lost son*, or something ob dat sort. Den I should have to lib wid dem, an' dey 'd want me to eat some 'spectable darkey's skin 'fore I knowed it, which I should n't like to do; so I tot it best, all day yesterday, to make for de bushes when-ebber I saw one ob those same colored gentl'men about here."

"Cuffee was afraid," said Baptiste, with a laugh.

"Jes' say dat again, little frog-eater, an' I 'll prove dat I ain't afraid ob you, any way."

"Come, come, Cuffee. This is Monsieur Bar-da's son; you must not be rude to him. He does not know you so well as I do, or he would not have said you were afraid," said Dick, the peace-maker.

"If dat am the case, I 'll excuse him dis once," said Cuffee, all the more readily for seeing that

Baptiste did not appear in the least afraid of him.

"Shall we go home now, Baptiste?" said Dick. "I want to put this truant before your father."

"Yes, we will go back now." replied Baptiste.

"Hold on, Massa Dick! You ain't a going fru those woods, are you?" asked Cuffee, uneasily.

"Yes," was the reply.

"If you do, you won't come out ob dem whole, dat's all."

"Why not?"

"'Cause you won't. I've been in dem an' I know. Dare are wultures dare dat would n't make nuffin' of eating us all at one meal."

"Vultures!" said Dick, incredulously.

"Yes Golly, did n't dey come after me by de dozen, an' nearly tore my eyes out! An' some ob them frew a big cocoa-nut down on my head; an' if this darkey's skull had been one inch thinner he would hab been a goner, sure. As it was, de cocoa-nut was a goner; and it made such a noise when my head hit it, dat de wultures tot dey were shot, an' dey all flew away. Den I picked up de pieces of cocoa-nut an' walked slowly out of dem woods. resolved nebber to go in dem again Tink ob de tears my poor mudder would shed if dey had killed me."

"Ha, ha!" laughed Baptiste. "Ze tern!"

"Yes," said Dick. "There is not a vulture in these woods, Cuffee. I suppose you were chased by a tern."

"By a tern; I tell you dare was a dozen ob dem, whatebber dey were. Dey may be call 1 tern, for all I know. If dey be, dey are well named; for dey made me turn, mighty sudden. But what can you say about de *spiders* dare are in dem woods?"

"Spiders?" said Dick and Baptiste together.

"Yes. Spiders a foot long chased me, hissing an' spitting, dare legs rattling like a bag of bones!"

"O, Cuffee!" said Dick, laughing.

"Ze land-crabs," said Baptiste.

"Are there land-crabs in these woods?" asked Dick.

"Yes, many. Zey often chase me."

"O, golly! 'Spect I'm goin' to beliebe dat? De wultures are nuffing but tern, an' de spiders are nuffing but crabs! Den de woods are *haunted!* else who fru de cocoa-nut?"

"No one did," replied Dick, laughing. "You were under the tree, I suppose, at the time, and it dropped on your head."

"Ob course it dropped on my head; but who *dropped* it? Dat's what I want to know."

"It dropped of its own accord. When cocoa-nuts are ripe, they fall to the ground."

A Surprise. — Page 67.

" O, dey do. Knowing tings dey must be.
But it's mighty funny how dat one knew enough
to fall on dis chile's head," said Cuffee, rubbing
the place where it struck, and appearing not quite
satisfied with the explanation.

After he had been provided with a stick, the
three boys began to make their way through the
woods.

Perhaps the birds and crabs thought their ene-
my too formidable now to attack; for the sticks
were not called into use all the way, much to
Cuffee's disappointment, who wanted to pay them
back in their own coin.

In half an hour they had reached Monsieur
Barda's house, and Cuffee was surrounded by the
family, who listened to his story with wonder and
amusement. They then had a dinner prepared
for him, that warmed his heart towards them all.

# CHAPTER X.

### TURTLE CATCHING.

It was a hot, sultry day, — too hot and sultry to be comfortable on the little island. The waves washed lazily upon the white sands, and the birds flew drowsily from tree to tree, too indolent to prolong their song beyond a quick " chirp."

Dick had wandered off alone, and had fallen asleep under the shade of a large banyan tree, and was dreaming of home and Daisy and Grandfather Milly.

Do all my young readers know how a banyan tree grows? If not, I will tell them, while Dick is dreaming.

From the tree, shoots drop to the ground, and form new stems, till a single tree becomes a grove. One of these trees, near the Narbudda River, in Hindostan, is described as covering an area of two thousand feet in circumference.

The one Dick was under, however, was not so large as that.

As he is not likely to awake for some time, I

will take this opportunity to tell my young readers something more about the vegetation of the torrid zone.

All of you know, I am sure, that in no other zone does it reach such a high development, not only in species, but also in luxuriance of growth.

Trees grow to a gigantic size, both in trunk and leaves, and upon them and among them flourish other plants, so that a tropical forest is often impenetrable.

Flowers of the most brilliant hues blossom in profusion in the forest, and float upon the inland waters.

What would my young readers say at the sight of a flower *three feet in diameter?* Such an one blossoms in the East India Islands, and is called the *Rafflesia.* And in tropical America is found the beautiful *Victoria Regia.* The blossom is white and rose-colored, is fifteen inches broad, and expands amid enormous leaves.

Ferns, also, which are mere herbs in the temperate regions, grow to the size of trees there; some of them twenty feet in height.

In the torrid zone, there are many species of *palms;* some of them two hundred feet high.

The different kinds yield cocoa-nuts, dates, sago, sugar, flour, wax, oil, healing balsam, and edible fruit resembling the cabbage.

I have told you before that the leaves are used in covering the roofs of dwellings; they are also used in making hats and fans. The wood is of excellent quality, and suited to many purposes.

The fibrous portions of the trunk and of the cocoa-nut husks are spun into thread and ropes; and the cocoa-nut shells are formed into cups and pipe-bowls.

Thus you see the palm surpasses every other plant in usefulness to man.

Now, we will return to Dick, asleep under the banyan tree.

He might have slept longer had it not been for Cuffee, who discovered his retreat, and awoke him without ceremony.

"Massa Dick! Wake up, an' come an' see de old women catching shrimp"

Dick rubbed his eyes and awoke, not at all pleased at having a pleasant dream destroyed.

"You must have a salamander constitution, Cuffee, to want to walk such a day as this is," said he.

"It *am* rudder hot, dat's a fac'; but dis chile hab a *motive* in walking about lively on such days."

"O, you have," said Dick, lazily.

"Yes. De fac' am, dis chile hab a friend in Boston, who has de misfortune to hab to work in a bake-house. I always drop in to see him, when I am in town, to condole wid him an' to eat some ob his sweet buns. *He* am always glad to see me, but de boss baker is n't  'Spect it 's cause I don't pay for de buns. He am a big fat man, wid more flour on him dan he ebber put in a ten-cent loaf. An *he* says dat I ain't *half baked*. 'Spect he can say dat when we meet again, if I sun myself many such days as dis am?"

" What did he mean by that?" asked Dick, laughing at Cuffee's serious expression.

" Dun know; unless he tinks I got burnt black outside too quick, an' did n't get done fru. But come, I want you to see de women catching shrimps."

Dick arose reluctantly, and followed him to a slightly elevated spot, where they had a fine view of the beach.

Four negro women could be seen catching shrimps, and their method of catching them was as novel as it was simple.

Two of them threw shells out into the water, which caused the shrimps to flock towards th? land; then the other two women would scoop them up.

" O, dear !" said Dick, yawning; " is *that* all there is to be seen? It is n't worth leaving my nice nest under the banyan tree for."

" I did n't get you out here to see *dem*," said
Cuffee, placidly.

" You did n't?"

" No; I wanted to wake you up, for I hab got
somefing to tell you dat you could n't 'preciate if
you 's half asleep."

" I shall not appreciate it, whatever it is, while
standing here in the hot sun; so we may as well
go back to the tree again," replied Dick, walking
towards the banyan tree.

" I nebber knew anyting to run away on account ob de sun before, unless it *was* an icicle,"
remarked Cuffee, scratching his head thoughtfully,
and following Dick.

" Now what is it that you want to tell?" said
the latter, after he had regained his former seat.

" Well, dat little frog-eater told me — "

" I wish you would not call my friend Baptiste
names. It is very wrong and unkind of you,
Cuffee, when Monsieur Barda is so good to you,
too," interrupted Dick, reproachfully.

" Who 's calling him names?" said Cuffee, dog-
gedly.

" You are. Did n't you just call him little frog-
eater?"

"Well, dat 's natural enuff, speaking ob a French
boy. Why don't you tell him to stop calling
*dis chile* names?"

" He never does."

" Yes, he does. He calls me Coffee. 'Spect I 's goin' to stan' dat? My name 's no more Coffee dan his is Tea."

" You know he means no offence. He can't speak your name any plainer."

" Well, it *sounds* de same as if he meant offence, anyway. But I was going to tell you dat he says dare will be a great time on de beach to-night, for de men are going to catch turtles."

" Catch turtles ? "

" Yes. If you had n't been so 'fraid ob your complexion you might have seen de darkies on de beach throwing up de sand in hills, to hide behind."

This information had the effect of rousing Dick from the state of *ennui* into which the hot weather had thrown him, and he hastened away to seek Baptiste, to learn from him if it were true

Baptiste was feeding his chameleon when Dick found him, and he answered in the affirmative ; saying that, "As soon as ze moon is high ze turtles will go on ze beach to lay zare eggs in ze sand."

That afternoon was a long one to Dick and Cuffee. It seemed an age before they, with Baptiste, were on the beach, kneeling behind a sand-hill, in the light moonlight, waiting for the turtles to make their appearance.

A row of sand-hills were on each side of them, and behind each one crouched a dark form.

Baptiste had told his two companions that they must wait till a turtle approached their hills, when one of them might creep out, and, getting between it and the water, secure it by one of its "flappers," and turn it upon its back, from which it could not arise. And he had repeatedly cautioned Cuffee to "be quiet," or the turtles would not come out of the water.

Before long the watchers heard a slight noise in the water at the right, and, looking in that direction, they saw a fine turtle making its way towards one of the sand-hills.

It paused when half-way between the hill and the water, and began to turn slowly around, making a hole in the sand with its flappers, in which to deposit its eggs.

While it was thus occupied, the dark form stole out from behind the hill, and, getting between it and the water, caught it by a flapper, and turned it upon its back.

All this Dick saw, and was turning to whisper something to Baptiste, when he heard an exclamation beside him, and saw Cuffee bounding over the top of the sand-hill, carrying half of it with him, and shouting in a shrill voice, —

"A chance for dis chile! A chance for dis chile!"

Of course, the turtle immediately took the alarm, and before Cuffee could reach it was in the water again. So he lost his " chance," and returned, looking rather sheepish.

He profited by the lesson, however, and the next time had better luck; for he succeeded in turning one upon its back, though not till after a long struggle between himself and it.

After two hours the boys returned to the house, loud in their praise of turtle catching, and the fun to be had thereat.

# CHAPTER XI.

### IN THE GRAVE-YARD.

THE next morning, while at breakfast, Monsieur Barda was interrupted by one of the negro women, who entered the house without ceremony, and said something to him hurriedly, crying bitterly all the while.

Dick could not understand what she said, but Baptiste told him that her little child was very sick, and that she wanted his father to visit it immediately.

Dick knew before that Monsieur Barda was the doctor, the minister, judge, jury, and lawyer of the island; but this was the first time he had been called upon to perform any of those duties since Dick had been there, excepting every Sunday morning, when he offered up a short prayer in French, upon the lawn, surrounded by his family, and those among the negroes who could understand him.

He did not stop to finish his breakfast, but went immediately with the woman, soon returning with

the information that the child was dead, and that
he had ordered work to be deferred for the day.

He then brought into the house a large sheet of
lead, which, after measuring and ruling, he formed
into a square box for the coffin  In it the child
was put; and towards evening it was borne, between four men, followed by all the men, women,
and children on the island, to the burying-ground.

Monsieur Barda dug the grave, and lowered the
coffin in it; then a man approached him, with four
ripe cocoa-nuts, which he took and planted, two at
the head and two at the foot of the coffin; he then
threw in the earth and trampled it down, and then
offered up a short prayer.

Dick had noticed, when he entered the burying-
ground, that there was not a sign of a stone, or
even a wooden slab, to mark the graves.  Nothing
but cocoa-nut trees, in every stage of growth, were
to be seen.  And they sprang up in regular order,
four being always of the same size.

So when he saw Monsieur plant the nuts, he
knew that every four trees marked a grave.

Turning to Baptiste, who was standing by his
side, he said: —

"Many people have died on your island, to
judge by the number of graves I see."

"Zey did not all die on ze island," replied
Baptiste.  "Many ships go down in ze fearful

storms, an ze dead bodies are washed ashore; an' often ships leave sick sailors here who die. My fazer buries zem all, an' when ze trees are big enough, he marks on zem ze flag of ze nation to which ze one zat is buried under zem belongs. We will go among ze trees an' see how zey are marked, when my farzer goes away."

Dick found that what Baptiste had said was true; for the flags of many nations were rudely carved in the trunks of the trees. He could not help feeling sad as he walked among them; and when his eyes rested upon the American flag, he thought that perhaps in dear New England, a father, mother, sisters, and brothers were waiting and watching, year in and year out, hoping against hope, and praying for the safe return of the one that lay beneath his feet turned to dust.

O, if he could only learn the names of those that were buried beneath the American flag, he might try, when he reached home, to find those who mourned for them. But no. The names had not been remembered, if they had ever been heard; and their fate must ever remain a mystery.

Dick turned sadly from the spot, feeling that it was a burying-ground indeed; for with the bodies were buried their names and fate forever.

# CHAPTER XII.

## A LETTER HOME.

MANY vessels arrived at the island while Dick was there. Some put in for repairs, and others for oil and provisions. By all those that were homeward bound he sent letters to Daisy, Grandfather Milly, Jack, Ella, and Bill Redcliff.

As soon as one package of letters had been sent, he would write others, so he always had some ready for every homeward-bound vessel.

One pleasant day, he was in his little room in the Frenchman's house, seated upon his trunk, with his small writing-desk in his lap, writing to Daisy.

The soft, warm winds blew in through the lattice window, sending in sweet fragrance from the blossoming vines without, as he wrote the following words : —

" DEAR SISTER DAISY :

Day before yesterday Monsieur Barda proposed visiting the next island. Of course, all were delighted with the idea, and your brother Dick was more so than any one.

At four o'clock yesterday morning, we (Monsieur Barda and his family, Cuffee and myself, and six negro men to row) got into the big boat, and started down the bay.

After four hours' rowing, we arrived at Monsieur Cailland's plantation. It appeared to be very much like the one I had just left, as I walked up the beach. Monsieur Cailland himself came running down to meet us. He was a little old Frenchman, dressed in the French style of many years ago, and looked exactly like the men pictured out in the old history at home, with his long periwig and knee breeches.

He kissed Monsieur Barda, and seemed overjoyed to see us all. He talked a great deal of French, and more broken English; but the most I could understand, he talked so fast, was, " We'll have ze fatte peeg;" meaning we would have roast pig for dinner.

On entering the house I was introduced to his wife, and two daughters, who all looked and dressed alike, in very short-waisted dresses, and very stiff, white caps.

While the old people were talking together, Baptiste and I went out for a walk. The island is so near like Diego Garcia, it would be worth while to describe it here.

I gathered some handsome shells, and some ripe seeds for you to plant when I get home.

You should see the lot of curiosities I have in my trunk for you. I had to take out all my books to make room for them. The books I gave to the Frenchman's children, and you should have seen their joy at the gift. They cannot read them, but most of their time every day is spent in looking at the pictures. If they could only have a copy of Mother Goose's Melodies, they would think it the most wonderful book ever printed. I told them some rhymes from it, and they were so pleased with them, they made me repeat them, until they learned to say them themselves.

It would make you laugh to hear them, while at play, singing,

> " Hoi, deedal, deedal, ze cat in ze fedal,
>   Ze cow jumped over ze moon,
> Ze leetal dog laft to see ze sport,
>   An ze deesh ron away wiz ze spoon."

I have not labelled any of the flower seeds i have gathered, for I thought if they ever came to anything you could give them prettier names than they have here. But I am wandering away from my visit to the island.

After Baptiste and I returned from our walk, we did justice to a splendid dinner that was served up out-doors, under a roof of cocoanut-tree leaves. After dinner, the Frenchman's two daughters played upon a guitar, and sang for us in French. They asked me to sing with them, but I begged to be excused, for my voice is not in a musical condition. In fact, it is *changing*, and it sounds very much like a big bass drum that serenaded me on my arrival.

At six o'clock we were all in the boat again, starting for home, and reached there by moonlight, having passed a very pleasant day.

I nearly forgot to tell you that Baptiste has taught me how to swim, and I am now nearly as good a swimmer as he is himself.

I have now been here four weeks, and I look for the "Andromeda" every day. I shall feel glad and sorry when I leave the island. Glad, for I long to be " homeward bound," and sorry at leaving so many kind friends forever. Baptiste gave me his pet chameleon, as a parting present from him, and he was quite offended because I refused to take it, until I succeeded in convincing him that it would not live long if I should take it, for I could get it no insects in winter for food.

This may be the last letter that I shall write on this island ; but you will receive many more from me before you see me ; for the captain said we must go to England before we cross the ocean, and we will stop at many seaports on the way. I

shall write to you from Mauritius, and from St.
Helena, and will give you a faithful description
of the Tower of London, for Captain Fairweather
has promised to take me there. Cuffee is calling
me, so good-by for the present.

Your loving brother,

Dick."

# CHAPTER XIII.

## GOOD—BY TO THE ISLAND.

MASSA DICK, Massa Dick! Look hard, now, an' tell me what you tinks dat am?" Dick had joined Cuffee on the beach, and, looking seaward, he saw a vessel dropping anchor in the harbor.

"It looks like —" began Dick, excitedly.

"It *am* de ' Andromeda.' Now what you tinks 'll become ob dis chile?"

"Why, what do you mean, Cuffee?" asked Dick.

"What do you tink de captin 'll do to me for jumping out ob dat ship?"

"Will he do anything?"

"Golly, you don't know de captin! He's worse dan wultures, spiders, an' land-crabs, when his temper's up! An' I'm tinking it'll *be* up, when he sees dis chile here, alibe an' fat, after he hab gone to de trouble ob shedding tears on account ob his def. Golly, how I wish I hadn't told you all dat I jumped out ob de winder a-purpose!"

" What difference would that have made?"

" Den I might say I *fell* out *accidentally* while polishing de cabin winders, an' would have been drowned, only I caught hold ob de hind leg ob a clam, which pulled me ashore, or someting ob dat sort. But now I am at de mercy ob de whole ob you. Golly, won't dis poor chile hab to catch it ! "

" Never fear, Cuffee. I 'll tell the captain just how it was ; and he won't say a word to you, I know, when he hears how near you did come to being drowned."

" If you only *will* put in a good word for dis chile, Massa Dick ! Don't forget to say dat I was polishing de winders. Unless you say dat, de captin 'll rile up anyway. I 'll leave it all to you ; an' if you *do* get dis darkey safe out ob de scrape, you 'll know who to go to when you want somebody to — do anuder good turn for." So saying, Cuffee hurried to the woods, thinking it best to be invisible until Dick had paved the way for him.

Soon a boat approached the shore from the ship, in which were three men ; and Dick, recognizing the captain as one of them, took off his cap and waved it in the air. Captain Fairweather immediately responded in a like manner.

By that time Monsieur Barda had discovered that the " Andromeda " had arrived, and came hurrying down to the beach to welcome his friend, the captain.

Baptiste came also, but his face expressed anything but joy at the sight of the ship, for he knew it would soon bear away the only playfellow of his own age he had ever known.

After the greetings had been said, the Frenchman hurried home to give orders for a more substantial welcome than words leaving the captain and Dick to follow at their leisure.

" I have sad news for you, Dick," said the captain, the first to speak after the Frenchman left them.

" What is it?" asked Dick, well knowing that he referred to Cuffee's supposed fate.

" My poor little cabin-boy, whom you took such a liking to, met a sad fate the first day out from the island. If you remember, I sent him into the cabin, while bidding you good-by. I did not go down myself for some time after, but when I did, the cabin window was open, and Cuffee not visible. Whether he jumped into the water, or fell in, I cannot say. I only know that the poor fellow was drowned, without a doubt."

" Why are you so positive? Could he not have swum ashore?" asked Dick.

" Impossible! The distance was too great. It is many years since I have had cause to feel so bad as I felt the day we learned that he was missing."

"But he was *only missing* after all, captain. What would you say if you should see him alive and well upon this island?"

"Dick, your face tells me that you know more about Cuffee's disappearance than I do. I thought it strange you were not more surprised Tell me, *was* I mistaken, after all? Is he alive?" said the captain, eagerly.

"He *is* alive, and was on this very spot not ten minutes ago; but he has taken to the woods now, in fear of a scolding from you for leaving the 'Andromeda.'"

"He is on this island, is he?" said the captain, slowly, his manner wholly changed.

"Yes, sir; and as lively as ever," replied Dick, much relieved, not understanding the change in the captain.

"O, he is! He'll be *livelier* than ever when I put my hands on him; you can bet your topmast on that," was the cool reply.

"You will not punish him, will you?" asked Dick, anxiously.

"Why not? Wasn't he the means of keeping the 'Andromeda' in a state of confusion for days? She might have gone to the bottom, for all the good I was able to do for her, on account of him.

And now he turns up here as *lively as ever*, and is not to be punished!"

"I am sure you will not punish him when you know all the poor fellow has suffered. I told you that he was afraid of the cholera, when I was on deck. He was *so* afraid of it that he ran the risk of being drowned rather than go where it is. He *was* nearly drowned, and was washed ashore, insensible, on the other side of the island. And not knowing where he was, he lived two days in the bushes near the beach, in constant terror for fear he had been cast upon a cannibal island."

"Served him right, too," replied the captain, with much satisfaction.

"I want you to promise me that you will not punish him. I am sure you said many times, while you thought he was dead, that if you could see him *alive*, you would never speak a cross word to him again"

"I *did* say some nonsense to that effect," replied the captain, visibly softening.

"Say that you will not punish him for this offence." urged Dick, seeing the advantage he had gained.

The captain was silent for a few moments, and walked two or three steps towards the beach, then returning, said, —

"I will promise, on this condition, that for the very next offence, I shall punish him for both."

"Thank you, sir," replied Dick, feeling certain that Cuffee would be careful of giving offence for a long time.

"Now, where is the little heathen?"

"Here I is, Massa Captin. I's mighty glad to see you!" said Cuffee himself, stepping out from behind a tree within five feet of them, where he had been listening to the conversation, and shaking his fist at the captain when it did not sound favorable to him, taking care the while not to be seen.

"You have been listening!" said the captain, angrily.

"'Deed, Massa Captin, I got behind dat tree accidently; an' when I saw you coming up, I did n't like to leave, for fear you might see me an' tink I's a ghost."

"You heard all that we said?"

"Ebery word, Massa Captin."

"You know, then, that to Dick, here, you are indebted for a whole skin."

"'Deed, Massa Captin, he did n't half do his duty. He did n't say nuffin' about how I was polishin' de cabin winder when I fell out."

"I can imagine that. Now remember, for the

very next offence you will receive double punishment."

" Dat's very kind ob you, captin, an' I's much obliged," replied Cuffee, innocently.

Captain Fairweather looked sternly at him, but saw only a very demure little black face.

By that time, Monsieur came with the information that dinner was waiting, and as the ship was to sail again in two hours, no more time must be lost.

After dinner, Dick went into the room that had been his so long, to pack his things in his trunk.

Baptiste went with him, for he could not lose sight of him the little time there was to see him.

"O. if I could only write, Deck, we might talk to each other across ze ocean," said he, sadly.

" I wish you could, or had some one to teach you," replied Dick. " But we will hear from each other often, for Captain Fairweather makes many voyages here ; and every time you see the ' Andromeda ' anchor in the harbor you may expect to hear from me. I will send you books with prettier pictures than those you have. I only wish I could come with them, to tell you about them."

" I shall hope zat every ship will be ze ' Andromeda,' for when it goes away I will send ze fruit to you."

" I shall be pleased to receive fruit that grew

on this island. Now, will you help me take the trunk down to the beach?"

Baptiste took hold of it readily; but to their consternation, as soon as it was lifted the bottom fell out, and all the contents were scattered over the floor.

"What is the meaning of that?" exclaimed Dick; for it was a good, strong trunk, and had seen but little use.

"Ah, ze white ants!" cried Baptiste, raising his hands.

"White ants?" replied Dick.

"Yes, ze ants have eaten it; see!" And Baptiste, taking up a piece of the bottom board, showed that it was hollow, a species of ant having eaten the inside of the board, leaving a thin layer of wood on the top and bottom, which of course gave way when the trunk was lifted.

Monsieur Barda provided Dick with an old chest, and with Baptiste's help the things were soon packed in it, and it was on its way down to the beach.

Fortunately, it was larger than his trunk had been, or it would never have held the many things that found their way into it; for it had to be opened many times before Dick and Baptiste succeeded in getting it down to the water. All the children had something to put in it as parting

7

presents, and many of the negroes; last of all, old Aunt Stagger, who came running down to the beach with a dish full of honey cakes; and though she could not speak a word of English, she made him understand by gestures that she was sorry he was going, as she placed the cakes carefully in the trunk.

Dick shook her hand heartily, and after bidding all good-by, sprang into the boat with Captain Fairweather and Cuffee.

The latter's appearance caused much astonishment among the sailors on board the "Andromeda." But after the captain had told them how Cuffee's life had been saved, and his object in jumping overboard, their astonishment changed to merriment, and many a joke was cracked at the cabin-boy's expense; but Cuffee took them all good-naturedly, even those that referred to his courage, saying, "It's true enuff, dis chile could n't face de cholera any more dan a codfish could shinny up a greased pole tail first."

# YOUNG AMERICANS IN THE WONDERFUL CITY OF TOKYO.

### Further Adventures of the Jewett Family and their Friend Otto Nambo.

#### By EDWARD GREEY,

Author of "Young Americans in Japan," "The Golden Lotus," etc. With one hundred and sixty-nine illustrations. Royal octavo, 7 x 9½ inches, with cover in gold and colors, designed by the author, $1.75. Cloth, black and gold, $2.50. Royal octavo, 7 x 9½ inches.

In the great city of the great Empire of Japan, which the Japanese themselves call wonderful, the Young Americans find new cause for wonder at the strange customs and curious sights. Under the guidance of "Oto Nambo," their stanch friend, they assist at a fire, dine at Tokyo restaurants, are entertained by amateur performers, visit all the points of interest, and meet with many adventures; but the most interesting part of the book to American boys will be the visits to and descriptions of the different trades, many of which are illustrated, and all of which are described, from the "seller of folding fans" to the maker of "broiled bean curd."

# YOUNG AMERICANS AMONG THE BEAR WORSHIPPERS

Of Japan, Yezo and the Island of Karafuto. By EDWARD
GREEV. Price, boards, $1.75; Cloth, $2.50.

Yezo formerly belonged to Japan, but was ceded to Russia in
1875. The people bear the same relationship to the Japanese as
the Indians do to America. They are as "hairy as bears, never
feel the cold, and live to be very aged." The various members
of the Jewett family and their friend, Oto Nambo, contrive to see
and tell a great deal of the manners, customs, sports, traditions,
and religion of this unknown and singular people. The book is
7 x 9½ inches; handsome cover; contains 180 illustrations by na
tive Japanese artists, and 304 pages. — *Herald of Truth.*

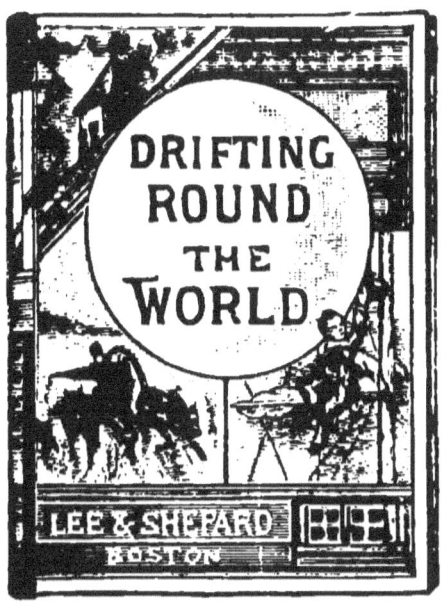

# DRIFTING ROUND THE WORLD.
## A Boy's Adventures by Sea and Land.

### By CAPT. CHARLES W. HALL,

Author of the "Great Bonanza," "Adrift in the Ice Fields," etc.

200 illustrations. 384 pages. Royal 4to. Illuminated sides, $1.75. Cloth, full gilt, $2.50.

This tells the story of a boy's adventures by sea and land with a spice of newness and interest that will commend it to the young and make it a favorite everywhere. It has some two hundred illustrations, and not a page that a boy would skip as he listens to the skipper tell his wonderful story. It is a splendid gift book.

# OUR BOYS IN INDIA.

**The Wanderings of Two Young Americans in Hindostan, with their exciting adventures, on the Sacred Rivers and Wild Mountains.**

### By HARRY W. FRENCH,

*Author of "OUR BOYS IN CHINA."*

With 145 illustrations. Royal octavo, 7 x 9½ inches. Bound in emblematical covers of Oriental design, $1.75. Cloth, black and gold, $2.50.

The great Indian Empire is the champion land for romance and adventure. In this story a little Yankee lad is kidnapped from his home. By the aid of a detective, an older brother, a lad of sixteen years, traces him to India. The adventures of the two, one as a captive and the other as a rescuer, in different parts of the empire, are thrilling, dealing as they do with the natives, the snake charmers and jugglers, royal personages and mountaineers, tiger hunts, elephant and rhinoceros fights. The descriptions of scenery, customs and wonders are graphic and instructive. Many of the illustrations are from special photographs taken for the author while in India. (27)

# OUR BOYS IN CHINA.

The thrilling story of Two Young Americans, Scott and Paul Clayton, wrecked in the China Sea on their return from India, with their strange adventures in China. By H. RRY W. FRENCH, author of "Our Boys in India." 150 illustrations. Royal 4to. Illuminated covers, $1.75. Cloth, back and gold $2.50.

"Our Boys in China" depicts the adventures of two young Americans wrecked in the China Sea on their return from India, with their romantic wanderings through the Chinese Empire. After successfully starting the young heroes of his previous book, "Our Boys in India," on their homeward trip, the popular and remarkable story-teller has them wrecked in the China Sea, saved and transported across China, giving him an opportunity to spread for young folks an appetizing feast of good things in the land of Confucius. — *Quincy Whig.*

# YOUNG AMERICANS IN JAPAN.

**Or, The Adventures of the Jewett Family and their
Friend Otto Nambo.**

### By EDWARD GREÉY.

With one hundred and seventy full-page and letter-press illustrations. Royal octavo, 7 x 9½ inches. Handsomely illuminated
cover, $1.75. Cloth, black and gold, $2.50. A new edition
of which is now ready.

Mr. Edward Greéy was a member of the famous expedition
which in 1854 caused "the Land of the Rising Sun" to be opened
to Eastern civilization. He afterwards returned to Japan, "living
among its estimable people, studied their language and literature,
and what they term, 'learned their hearts.'" He is thus qualified
to be a trustworthy guide to this the youngest and oldest of nations.
His pen-pictures of Japanese scenery and customs are graphic, and
by the introduction of spicy conversation are made dramatic. Mar-
kets and bazaars, shaké shops and Buddhist temples, jin-riki-shas
and jugglers are all brought before the eye.

(29)

# THE TIDE MILL STORIES.

Illustrated.   Each volume, 16mo, $1.25.

PHIL AND HIS FRIENDS.

THE TINKHAM BROTHERS' TIDE MILL.

THE SATIN-WOOD BOX.

THE LITTLE MASTER.

HIS ONE FAULT.

PETER BUDSTONE.

## LITTLE MISS WEEZY.
## LITTLE MISS WEEZY'S BROTHERS.
### By PENN SHIRLEY.
### CLOTH. ILLUSTRATED. 75 cts.

Little Miss Weezy must have been "brought up" with the whole tribe of "Little Prudy" folks, for though her story is decidedly original, she has cute ways, smart sayings, and an infinite variety of funny adventures equal to the best for which Sophie May is responsible.

# TEN BOYS.

By the author of " Seven Little Sisters," " Seven Little Sisters prove their Sisterhood," and " Geographical Plays." Cloth, $1.00.

In all my acquaintance with juvenile literature, I know of nothing in many respects equal to this remarkable book, which contains in its small compass the concentrated knowledge of vast libraries. It is the admirably told story of past centuries of the world's progress, and the amount of study and labor required in its preparation seems almost appalling to contemplate. One is struck with the peculiar excellence of its style, clear, easy, graceful, and picturesque, — which a child cannot fail to comprehend, and in which " children of a larger growth " will find an irresistible charm. That it will prove a favorite with old and young I have no doubt. It seems to me that nothing could be more enjoyable to the boy of our period than the story of how the boys of all ages lived and acted.

Yours truly,     JOHN G. WHITTIER.

# THE YOUNG WRECKER;

Or, the Trials and Adventures of Fred Ransom. By RICHARD MEADE BACHE. Illustrated. $1.00.

The Florida wreckers are not demons, luring ships to destruction with false lights, as has sometimes been erroneously believed; but brave, hardy men, who peril life to save, and whose adventures, as recorded in this book, are thrilling and surprising. It is a fine story, and the author's geographical and historical facts are as interesting as the story is entertaining.

(21)

# A BOSTON GIRL'S AMBITIONS.

### Cloth.   Price, $1.50.

Uniform in size and price with

**That Queer Girl.**

**Darryll Gap; or, Whether it Paid.**

**Only Girls.**

**A Woman's Word, and How She Kept It.**

**Lenox Dare.**

**But a Philistine.**

## THE HOLLAND SERIES.

By the same Author.  12mo.  Cloth, per Volume, $1.00
Comprising

**The Deerings of Medway.**       **Six in All.**
**The Mills of Tuxbury**        **The Hollands.**

These four are among Miss Townsend's best home stories, and have been out of print for some time.

---

## SIMPLICITY AND FASCINATION.

By ANNE BEALE.  Cloth, $1.00.  Regarded by the English critics as "one of the finest" modern novels published.  New Edition.